GRAMMAR RAY
A graphic guide to grammar
ADJECTIVES

Andrew Carter

alphabet
s o u p™
an imprint of
WINDMILL BOOKS™
New York

Published in 2010 by Windmill Books, LLC
303 Park Avenue South, Suite # 1280, New York, NY 10010-3657

Published by Evans Brothers Limited
2A Portman Mansions
Chiltern Street
London W1U 6NR
© in this edition Evans Brothers Limited 2010
© in the text and illustration Andrew Carter 2010

Adaptations to North American Edition © 2010 Windmill Books

CREDITS:
Written by: Andrew Carter
Editor: Sophie Schrey
Designer: Mark Holt

Library of Congress Cataloging-in-Publication Data

Carter, Andrew, 1979-
Adjectives / Andrew Carter. -- North American ed.
p. cm. -- (Grammar ray: a graphic guide to grammar)
Includes index.
ISBN 978-1-60754-737-2 (lib. bdg.) -- ISBN 978-1-60754-745-7 (pbk.) --
ISBN 978-1-60754-746-4 (6-pack)
1. English language--Adjective--Juvenile literature. 2. English language--Grammar--Juvenile literature. I. Title.
PE1241.C38 2010
428.2--dc22
2009041406

CPSIA Compliance Information: Batch #EWO1O2W: For further information contact Windmill Books, New York, New York at 1-866-478-0556.

Manufactured in China

contents

INTRODUCTION

Hello and welcome to Grammar Ray!
This book is a peek into a world of fun and
adventure, where English grammar is brought to life.
The English language gives words different jobs to do.
Each job is one of the "parts of speech."
This book explores the job that
adjectives do.

Hello! My name is Mr. Adjective.
I am on a mission to find the magician's
missing wand.

The first part of the book is a comic strip. Mr.
Adjective is on a quest to to solve the mystery
of the missing magic wand. He will meet some
interesting characters along the way. Look out
for the words in red – they are key to the story.

After you've followed Mr. Adjective's quest, the
rest of the book explains the role of adjectives in
more detail, and gives some more examples.
You can refer to this chart if you need a
reminder of how adjectives are used in English
grammar. Make sure you pay attention so you'll
become a whiz at spotting bright, colorful,
helpful adjectives whenever you see them!

Let's modify nouns

Adjectives are words that can tell us more about nouns. Before we take a closer look, let's remind ourselves what we know about nouns.

Nouns are the words we use to name things. For example:

a stage,

a magician,

a hat,

a rabbit,

a monkey,

some monkeys,

mischief,

panic.

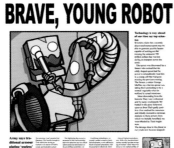

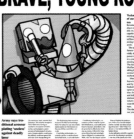

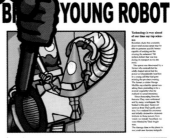

Adjectives are words that can tell us more about **nouns**.

A **red robot** was cleaning when a poster caught his eye.

Adjectives are often placed immediately in front of the **noun** they refer to, so they are easy to spot.

The robot had a **brilliant idea**...

...he used his **special key** to open the magician's **secret room**.

8

The magician's hat was on a tall table.

There was a bright light inside.

The robot peered over the edge and fell into the deep hole...

9

...down a long tunnel...

...and landed on some soft, green grass.

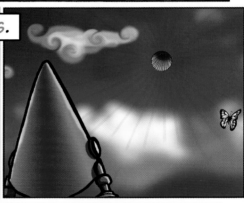

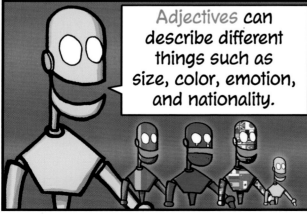

Adjectives can describe different things such as size, color, emotion, and nationality.

A small, white rabbit,

some happy rabbits.

Look!

The magic wand!

Words like "very" and "really" can be placed before adjectives to strengthen their meaning.

A *very* hard rock,

a *really* soft armchair,

a **very** tasty feast.

Adjectives can also be used to compare two or more nouns. For example:

a big carrot,

a bigger carrot,

the biggest carrot.

The magic wand turned them in to a huge pile of carrot pieces.

The hungry rabbits approached,

followed by...

...a big, mean hare.

By adding a hyphen (-) to certain words in a sentence, we can create compound adjectives. For example: a 'hare eating carrot'
(noun)   (verb)   (noun)

could become...

a hare-eating carrot.
(compound adjective)   (noun)

A kind-hearted rabbit helped the carrot-eating hare.

The robot had the magic wand, but how was he going to get home?

Clever rabbits...

...what a good idea!

...a wonderful surprise.

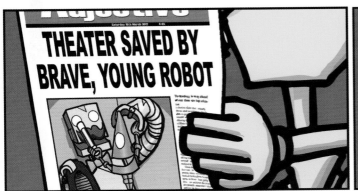

THEATER SAVED BY BRAVE, YOUNG ROBOT

The end

adjectives

**An adjective is a word that tells us more about a noun.
We can spot adjectives in a sentence easily because they are often placed
immediately in front of the noun they refer to.**

FOR EXAMPLE: *the <u>red</u> robot, a <u>large</u> carrot, <u>funny</u> people*

There are several types of adjective.

DESCRIPTIVE ADJECTIVES

Descriptive adjectives are the most common type of adjective. They describe the quality, state, or action of things and can tell us about size, color, shape, emotional state, and nationality.

FOR EXAMPLE: *a <u>large</u> dinosaur, a <u>small</u> house, a <u>giant</u> spider*

a <u>purple</u> flower, a <u>green</u> tomato, a <u>yellow</u> car

a <u>round</u> table, a <u>square</u> mirror, a <u>thin</u> boy

<u>happy</u> people, an <u>angry</u> rabbit, the <u>crazy</u> monkey

a <u>Japanese</u> fish, an <u>English</u> rose, an <u>African</u> zebra.

NUMERICAL ADJECTIVES

Numerical adjectives can show the number or order of things.

FOR EXAMPLE: **NUMBER:**
*<u>one</u> horse, <u>twenty</u> soldiers,
<u>one hundred</u> cookies, <u>each</u> person*

INDEFINITE NUMBER:
*<u>many</u> tigers, <u>several</u> mice,
<u>some</u> grass, a <u>few</u> options*

ORDER:
<u>first</u> place, <u>second</u> in command, <u>final</u> bell

comparing adjectives

Adjectives can be used to compare nouns.
Adjectives have three levels of comparison called the positive,
comparative, and superlative.

FOR EXAMPLE:

a <u>big</u> carrot
(POSITIVE)

a <u>bigger</u> carrot
(COMPARATIVE)

the <u>biggest</u> carrot
(SUPERLATIVE)

Let's look in a bit more detail.

POSITIVE

The positive shows the basic form of the adjective.

FOR EXAMPLE:

a <u>hot</u> country, a <u>wise</u> man, an <u>important</u> exam

COMPARATIVE

The comparative shows that the noun has more of the adjective quality than just the basic, or positive adjective. We use the comparative when we are comparing two things. To create a comparative we usually add −er to the end of the adjective. However this doesn't always work and you will be able to tell if the ending sounds wrong. For longer adjectives, for example, we use "*more*" before the word.

FOR EXAMPLE:

England was <u>hot</u>, but Spain was <u>hotter</u>.
He thought he was <u>wise</u>, but his sister was <u>wiser</u>.
The other exam was <u>more important</u>.

SUPERLATIVE

The superlative shows when the noun has the maximum amount of the adjective quality, above the level of the others. We use the superlative when we compare three or more things. To create a superlative we usually add –*est* to the end of the adjective. But, as with comparative adjectives, this doesn't always work. For longer adjectives in the superlative we use "*most*" before the word.

NOTE:

We use the article "*the*" when using the superlative.

FOR EXAMPLE:

Egypt was the hottest country.
He was the wisest of the three men.
This exam is the most important.

Some adjectives have irregular comparative and superlative forms.

FOR EXAMPLE:

good, better, best
many, more, most
bad, worse, worst
little, less, least

comparing adjectives

A compound adjective is formed when two or more adjectives work together to describe the noun. They are joined by a hyphen (-).

FOR EXAMPLE: *long-lasting, paper-thin, mouth-watering*

By adding a hyphen we can greatly change the meaning of sentence. Compound adjectives often mean something completely different than the original words they are formed from.

Let's look again at the example from the comic:

FOR EXAMPLE:

a hare   eating   carrot = a hare eating some carrot
(NOUN)   (VERB)   (NOUN)

a   hare-eating   carrot = a carrot that eats hares
    (COMPOUND)   (NOUN)
    ADJECTIVE

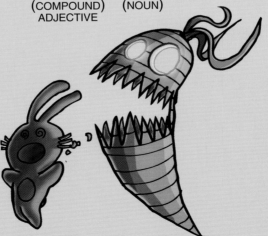

adjectives
Test yourself

Don't write in your Grammar Ray book. Please use a separate sheet of paper to test yourself!

1. Which two words in the following list are *not* adjectives?

lucky, orange, in, Dutch, smooth, run, few

2. Choose the adjectives to complete the sentence.*

A ------, ------- robot with

---, ------, ---- arms.

hot   red   big   lazy
yellow round triangular
square   blue   many

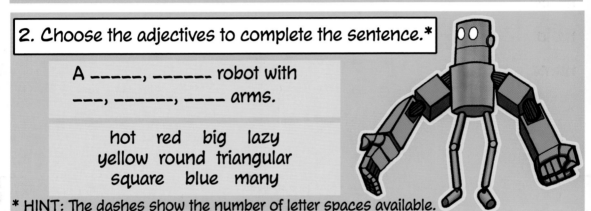

* HINT: The dashes show the number of letter spaces available.

3. Match the following words and pictures:
(a) four armed robots
(b) four-armed robots

1.

2.

Turn the page upside down to see the answers!

(1) in, run (2) A round, yellow robot with big, square, blue arms. (3) 1-a, 2-b

22

GLOSSARY

adjectives (ADD-jehk-tivz) words that tell you more information about nouns and pronouns

brilliant (BRILL-yant) very smart

compound (KOM-pownd) two things that combine to create one thing

emotion (ee-MOH-shun) a feeling

hare (hair) an animal like a rabbit with longer ears

mischief (MIST-shif) trouble

nationality (na-shun-NAL-ity) what country a person comes from

numerical (new-MEAR-ih-cull) having to do with numbers

INDEX